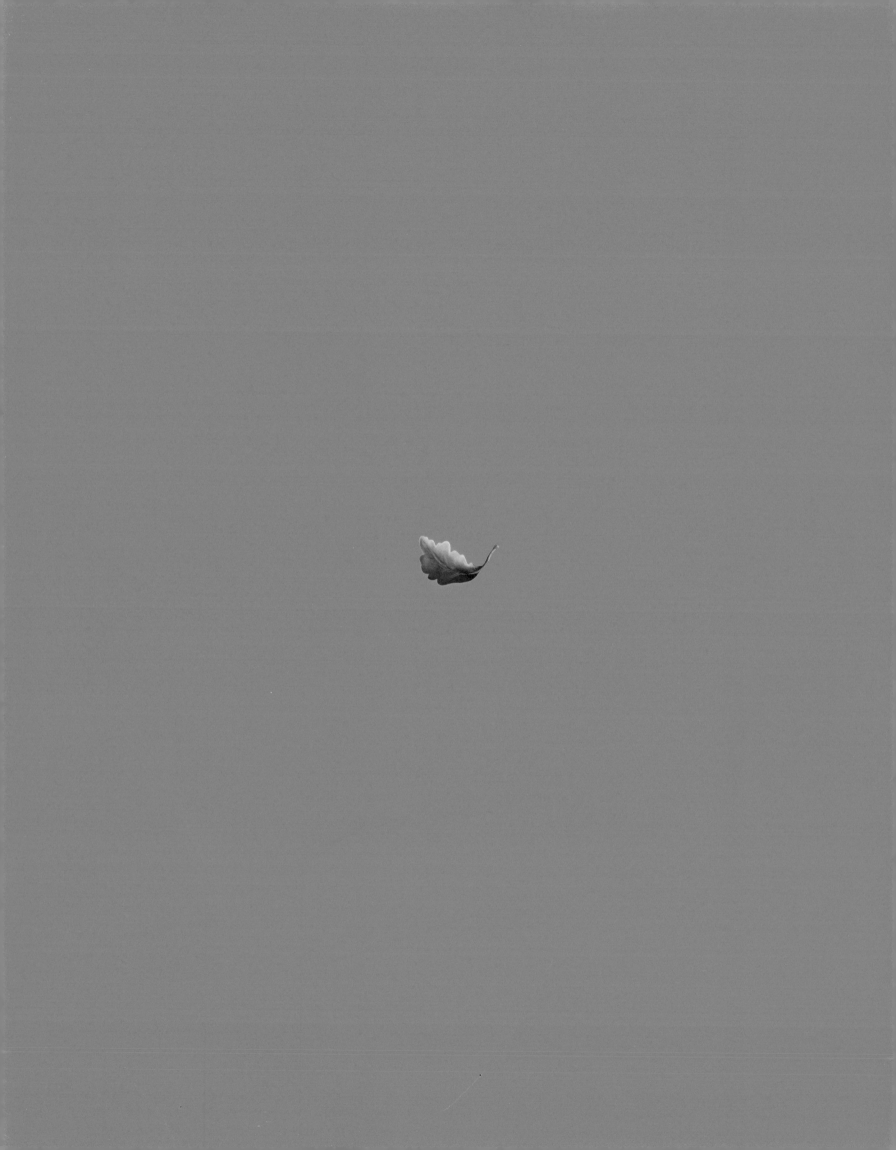

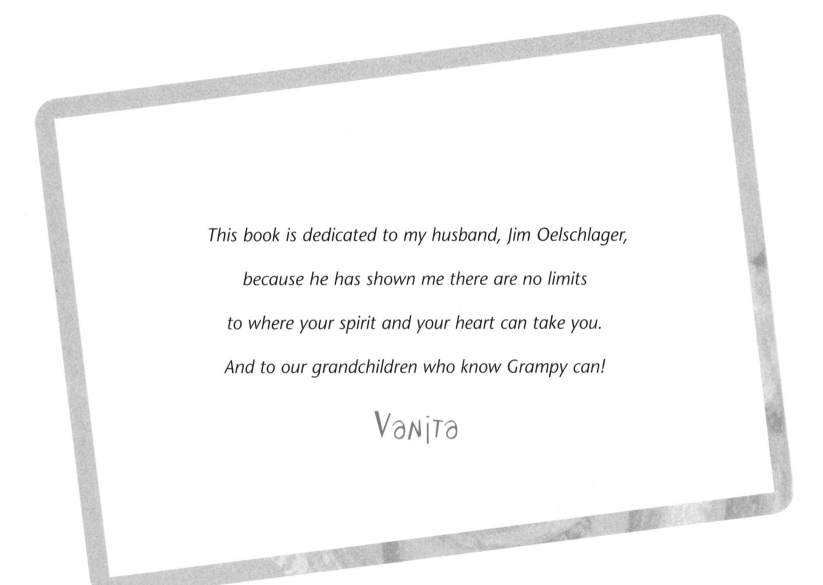

This book is dedicated to my husband, Jim Oelschlager,

because he has shown me there are no limits

to where your spirit and your heart can take you.

And to our grandchildren who know Grampy can!

Vanita

All proceeds from this book will be given to The Oak Clinic
for Multiple Sclerosis and The Mellen Center for Multiple
Sclerosis (Cleveland Clinic Foundation). I hope through their efforts,
and all those who are working to end the devastating effects of
multiple sclerosis, that within our lifetimes MS stands for "Mystery Solved."

Acknowledgements

Robin Hegan

Kristin Blackwood

Sheila Tarr

Trio Design

Mike Blanc

Dave Shoenfelt

My Muses

My Grandchildren

Cleveland Clinic Press

Austin Printing

My Grampy Can't Walk
Cleveland Clinic Press
All rights reserved.
© 2006 by Vanita Oelschlager
No part of this book may be reproduced in retrieval system or transmitted in any form or through
method including electronic, photocopying, online download or any other system now known or hereafter
invented – except by reviewer who may quote brief passages in a review to be printed in a newspaper
or print or online publication – without express written permission from the Cleveland Clinic Press.
Text by Vanita Oelschlager.
Illustrations by Robin Hegan and Kristin Blackwood.
The main illustrations were prepared in water mixable oils on wood panels.
The border illustrations were prepared in oil pastels and watercolor.
The text type was set in Stone Sans.
The display type was set in Big Fish Ensemble.
Designed by Trio Design & Marketing Communications Inc.
Photos by Dave Shoenfelt.
Printed on Mohawk Paper's Navajo, Brilliant White.
Printed by Austin Printing Inc.
ISBN 1-59624-015-6

For information, address Ultimate Acorn, Inc., c/o Oak Associates, ltd.
3875 Embassy Parkway, Suite 250, Akron, Ohio 44333-8355.

www.mygrampy.net

My Grampy Can't Walk

WRITTEN BY VANITA OELSCHLAGER

ILLUSTRATED BY ROBIN HEGAN AND KRISTIN BLACKWOOD

My Grampy can't walk.
He has Multiple Sclerosis
Which is a disease,
Or "MS" if you please.
He uses a wheelchair
To go fast as a breeze.

A BREEZE

LISTENS TO

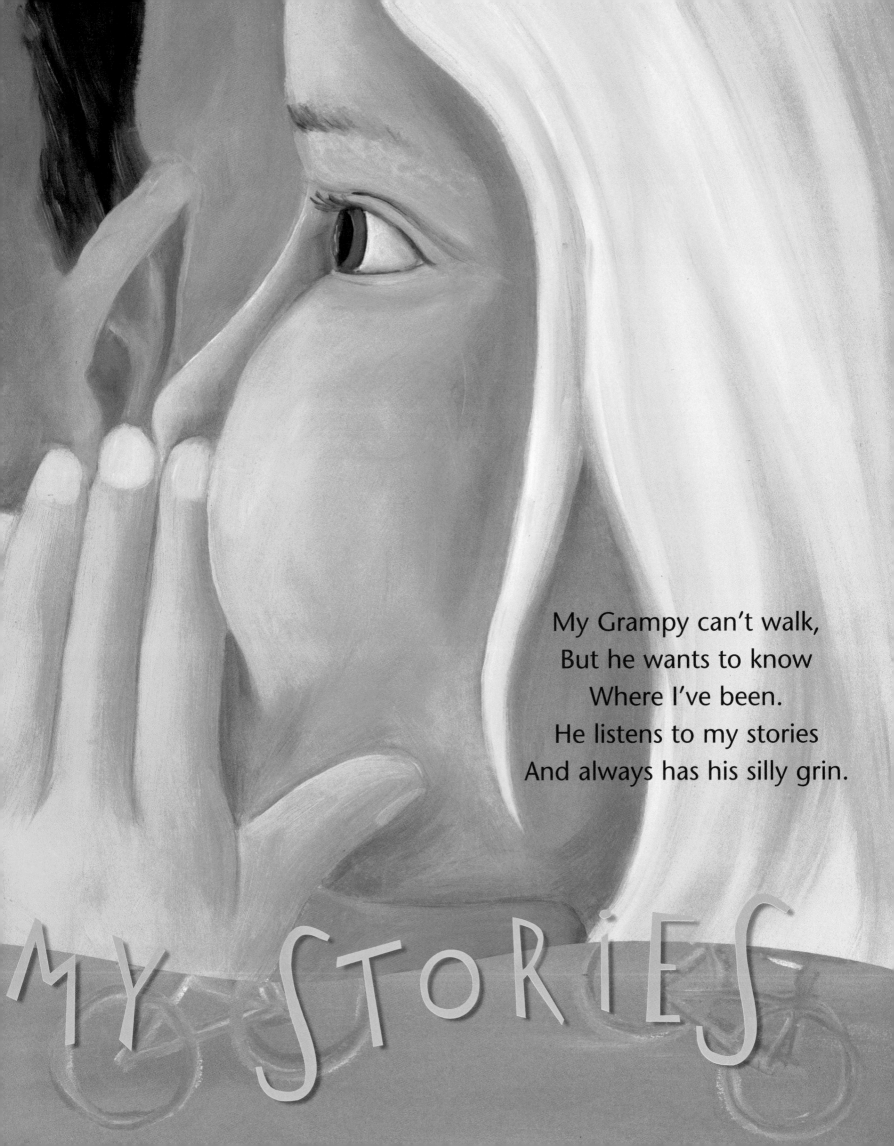

My Grampy can't walk,
But he wants to know
Where I've been.
He listens to my stories
And always has his silly grin.

MY STORIES

My Grampy can't walk,
But nothing misses his eye.
Now and then we'll just stop
And watch the changing sky.

NOTHING MIS

My Grampy can't walk.
But he can ride like the wind,
Like we're off to a race.
He can scoop me into his arms,
And we go off to our secret place.

TO OUR SEC

My Grampy can't walk.
But he can love me
From the top of my head
To the tips of my toes.
That includes my belly button,
My ears, my mouth
And my nose.

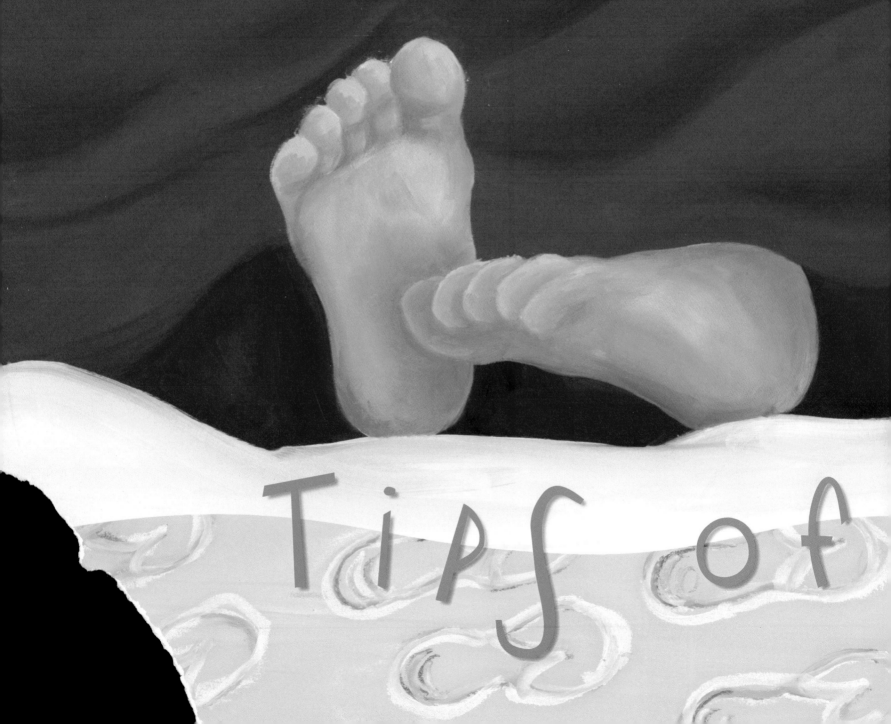

Tips of

MY TOES

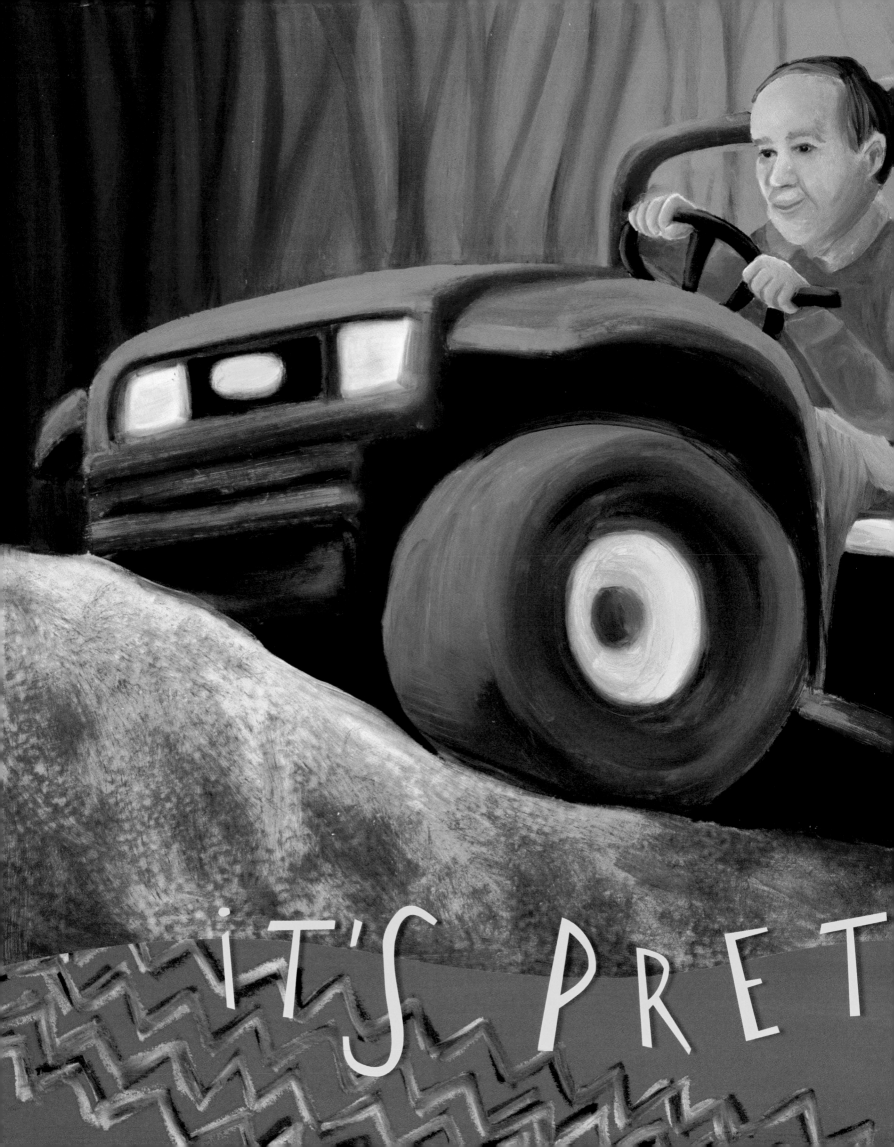

IT'S PRET

My Grampy can't walk.
But he can drive with his hands
And never use his feet.
Other people can't do that,
And I think it's pretty neat.

My Grampy can't walk.
But when we eat dinner with him,
Whether peanut butter or figs,
We can eat dessert first
And get dirty as pigs.

My Grampy can't walk.
But he can teach me about
Animals and rocks,
Clouds and
Something called "stocks."

My Grampy can't walk.
But he can fly
Through the sky
So high
We see his mashed potato clouds
Flying by.

MASHED POT

My Grampy can't walk,
But he works every day.
If you like your job,
He says it's like play.

WORK IS

LIKE PLAY

My Grampy can't walk.
But he takes me looking for bears
By the cave and the brook.
We haven't seen one yet,
But we always stop to look.

Looking

for BEARS

My Grampy can't walk.
But he can read to me
Stories of far-away places.
Or see who laughs first
When we make funny faces.

My Grampy can't walk,
But he thinks he's real funny.
When he tries to tell a joke
His eyes get all runny.

HiS EYES

My Grampy can't walk.
But he can make me
Laugh when I'm sad,
And feel better
When I've been bad.

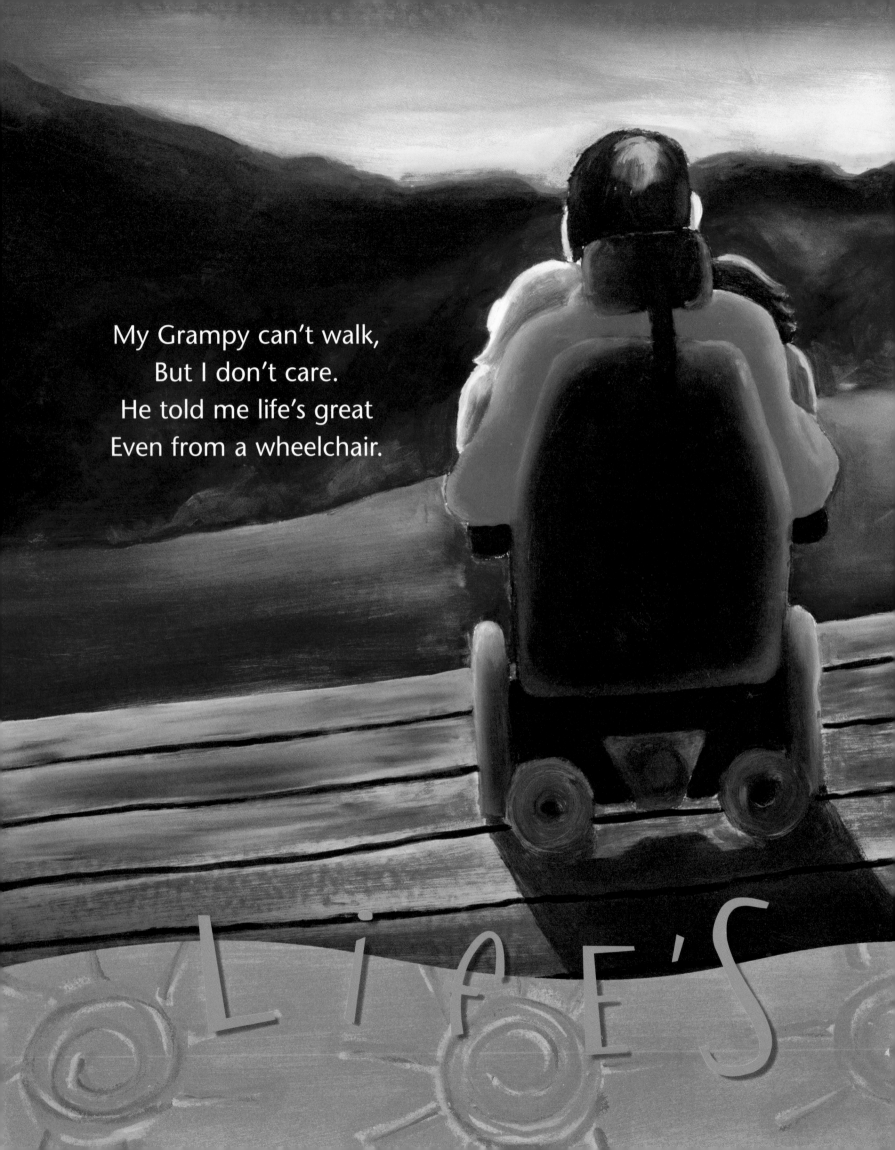

My Grampy can't walk,
But I don't care.
He told me life's great
Even from a wheelchair.

GREAT

Grampy and Grandkids

Grampy and Grammy

Grampy can't walk.
But he's a White Knight for sure.
He rode in to get me
Like the knights of yore.
His horse is different,
It's electric and steel.
But, for me, his machine
Is really a wonderful steed.

KIDS ABOUT GRAMPY

Anna

My Grampy can't walk.
When Grampy asks me
What I'm doing
And I say "not'in."
Then he asks me if I have
Chewing gum in my belly button.

Lily

My Grampy can't walk,
But he helped me to learn how.
I used his wheelchair
To pull myself up
And Grampy never cared.

Andrew

Tho' my Grampy can't walk,
We still go by the pond.
Sometimes, if we're lucky,
I catch a frog in my net.
We can touch it and talk to it
And look in its eyes.
Then Grampy always checks,
"Have you let it go yet?"

Abi

My Grampy can't walk.
But with me in his lap,
We can ride anywhere.
Zipping along paths in his woods
W-h-o-o-s-h
I feel the wind blow through my hair.

Sage

Grampy can't walk.
But he can let me crawl in bed with him
'Til he snores and kicks.
And when he has
A Dilly Bar,
He always gives me licks.

Vi-Yen

My Grampy can't walk.
But he helped me travel
From very far away,
To become part of a loving family
Every single day.

Author

Vanita Oelschlager This is Vanita's fifth book. She is a graduate of Mount Union College, where she is currently a member of the Board of Trustees. She has also taught in public schools throughout Ohio. When she isn't writing, Vanita works with "Grampy" – her husband, Jim – at Oak Associates, *ltd*. Together they have four children and six grandchildren.

Illustrator

Robin Hegan This is the second children's book she has illustrated. Robin is a graduate of The Pennsylvania State University with a degree in Integrative Arts. She resides in Ohio where she works at Oak Associates, *ltd*. At home, Robin enjoys illustrating and being with her husband and daughter.

Illustrator

Kristin Blackwood This is Kristin's second children's book. She has a degree from Kent State University in Art History. In addition to teaching and her design work, Kristin enjoys being a mother to her two daughters.